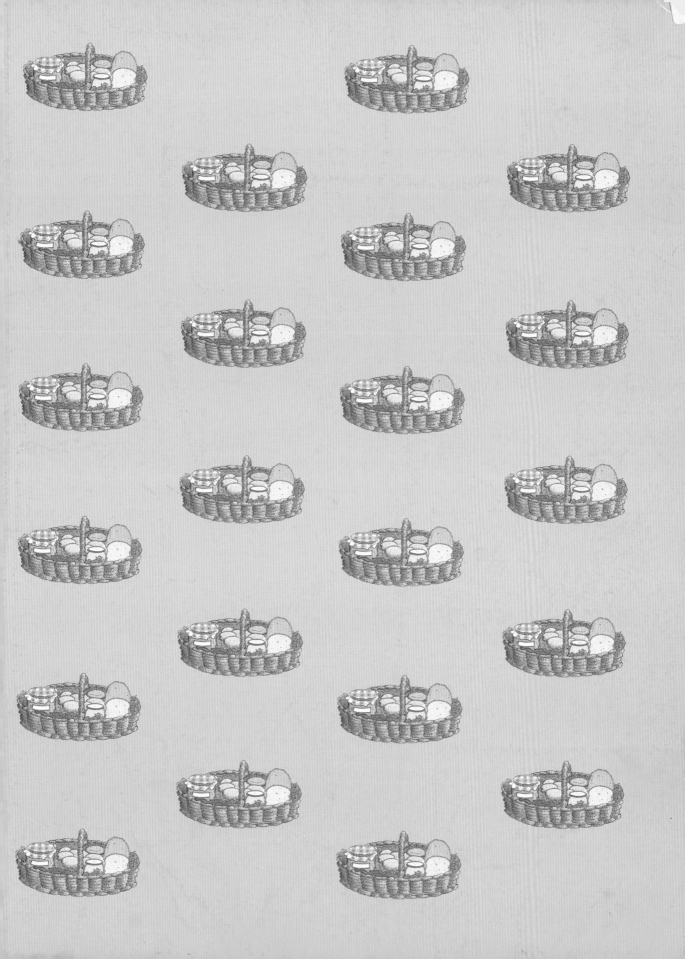

OXFORD
UNIVERSITY PRESS

Great Clarendon Street, Oxford OX2 6DP

Oxford University Press is a department of the University of Oxford.
It furthers the University's objective of excellence in research, scholarship,
and education by publishing worldwide in

Oxford   New York

Auckland   Cape Town   Dar es Salaam   Hong Kong   Karachi
Kuala Lumpur   Madrid   Melbourne   Mexico City   Nairobi
New Delhi   Shanghai   Taipei   Toronto

With offices in

Argentina   Austria   Brazil   Chile   Czech Republic   France   Greece
Guatemala   Hungary   Italy   Japan   Poland   Portugal   Singapore
South Korea   Switzerland   Thailand   Turkey   Ukraine   Vietnam

Oxford is a registered trade mark of Oxford University Press
in the UK and in certain other countries

First published 2002
Reissued with a new cover 2007

British Library Cataloguing in Publication Data

Data available

ISBN: 978-0-19-272498-4

7 9 10 8

Printed in Malaysia by Imago

Paper used in the production of this book is a natural,
recyclable product made from wood grown in sustainable forests.
The manufacturing process conforms to the environmental
regulations of the country of origin.

LITTLE RED RIDING HOOD

IAN BECK

OXFORD
UNIVERSITY PRESS

Once upon a time lived a girl called Little Red Riding Hood. She always wore a red cape with a hood that her grandmother had made for her. She lived with her mother in a house near a deep dark forest.

One morning her mother called her.

'Granny isn't well,' she said. 'Please take this to her.' And she gave Little Red Riding Hood a basket full of good things to eat. 'Now, mind you stay on the path,' said her mother. Little Red Riding Hood promised.

After a while she saw a woodcutter.
'Hello,' he called out cheerily. 'Off to see
your granny? Well, mind how you go.'

A little later she met a cunning and hungry
wolf. He was dressed in a green coat and was
leaning against a tree.

'Good morning, little girl,' he said politely. 'What's your name?'

But all the while he was thinking what a delicious meal she would make.

'Good morning,' said the girl. 'I'm called Little Red Riding Hood.'

And she tried to walk past on the narrow path.

'Wait,' said the wolf. 'What's in that basket?'

He lifted the cloth and saw all the good things underneath.

'Delicious,' he said. 'Who are they for?'

'They are for my granny,' said Little Red Riding Hood. 'She lives just over there.'

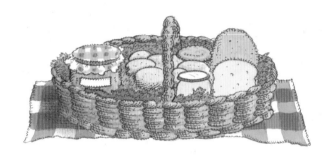

She pointed to Granny's cottage.

'Well,' said the sly wolf, 'don't you think Granny deserves some flowers as well?'

'I suppose it can't do any harm,' said Little Red Riding Hood, and she skipped off the path, into the bluebells, and deep into the wood.

Quickly, the wolf set off down the path to Granny's cottage.

The wolf tapped lightly on the door.
'Who's there?' called Granny.

'It's me,' the wolf replied in a little voice.
'It's Little Red Riding Hood. I've brought
you a lovely basket of things to eat.'

'Let yourself in, dear,' said Granny.

So the wolf lifted the latch.

He slipped into Granny's bedroom and,
before she could cry out for help, he
swallowed her up in one big gulp.

Then he put on her night-cap and
dressing-gown, and sat in her bed.
He pulled the covers up to his chin, so that
only a tiny bit of him was
showing, and then he
waited.

Soon there came a gentle tap-tap at the door.

'Who is it?' croaked the wolf.

'It's me, Granny,' said Little Red Riding Hood. 'I've brought some flowers and a basket of good things to eat.'

'Mmmm,' said the wolf. 'Just lift the latch and let yourself in.'

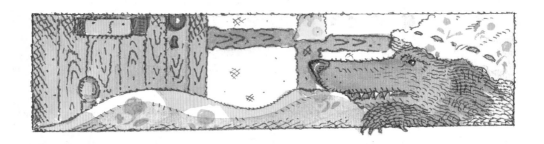

Little Red Riding Hood went into the cottage, and through to the bedroom. There she saw Granny looking much worse than she had imagined.

She went closer and sat by the bed.

'My goodness, Granny,' she said,
'what big eyes you have.'

'All the better to see you with, my dear,'
said the wolf.

'And, Granny,
what **big** ears you have,'
said Little Red Riding Hood.

'All the better to hear you with, my dear,'
said the wolf.

'And, most of all,
what **big teeth** you have,'
said Little Red Riding Hood.
'All the better to eat you with, my dear!'
cried the wolf, and he leapt out of Granny's bed.

'Help!' screamed Little Red Riding Hood.
'You're not my granny! Help! Help!'
The wolf chased her round and round the
little bedroom. He snarled and he snapped.
But at that very moment the door burst open.

There stood the woodcutter with his axe.
He struck one great blow, and the wolf
split in two.

Out tumbled Granny, safe and whole.

Little Red Riding Hood gave her granny the basket of good things, and the big bunch of bluebells. They all had a delicious supper, and then the woodcutter took Little Red Riding Hood home.

After that, Little Red Riding Hood always stayed on the path, and never spoke to strangers again.